LITTLE CRITTER®'S
THE TRIP

BY
MERCER MAYER

*To Arden Kay,
Doward, & Phillip*

inchworm
PRESS
™

A MERCER MAYER LTD. / J.R. SANSEVERE BOOK

Today we are going
on a trip.

I help Dad pack the car.

We drive through
the country.
Watch out for
the horse, Dad!

Look, Mom and Dad,
Kitty came too!
Surprise!

Uh-oh, Dad!
I think we are lost.

Drats!
Now there are too many cars!

Oh, no, Dad!
Now our car is too hot!

We drive and drive.
Little Sister and I play a game.

Then we get hungry,
so we stop for a snack.

Yum-yum! Our snack is good,
but it's a little messy, too.

Sorry, Mom!

We drive all day long.
It is getting dark.
Are we there yet, Dad?

Yikes!
Our tire is bad.

So I help Dad fix it.
Will we ever get there?

Hooray!
We are finally here…

…just in time for
a good night's sleep!